About the Author

David was born in 1952.
He married Diane in 1970. They have two daughters, six grandchildren and one great granddaughter.

David retired in 2017 and that's when he started to write children's stories. First of all for his grandchildren.
He enjoyed writing so much that he soon had a large collection of children's stories.
He has self-published some. David then started to write more adult stories, 'who done it' and the like.
David finds writing a great way of taking his mind off his arthritis.

TO DENNIS,

OUR GREAT FRIEND.

GOD BLESS
       DAVE + DIANE

Dedications

I would like to dedicate this book to my wife Diane.
Diane has been very patient and understanding with me spending many hours at my computer.

Also, I would like to dedicate it to my childhood friend Tony Denton.

David Charles Williams

WILL THE BIRDS EVER SING AGAIN?

AUSTIN MACAULEY PUBLISHERS™

LONDON • CAMBRIDGE • NEW YORK • SHARJAH

A CIP catalogue record for this title is available from the British Library.

ISBN 9781398407756 (Paperback)
ISBN 9781398416444 (ePub e-book)

www.austinmacauley.com

First Published (2021)
Austin Macauley Publishers Ltd
25 Canada Square
Canary Wharf
London
E14 5LQ

Imagine our world without birds.
The year is 2057 and the birds have stopped singing.

During the years since the 1950s, Earth has suffered from all sorts of mainly 'Man-Made' disasters.

However, the year is now 2057 and everything has come to a head.

Only one man, Professor Denton, it seems can save the world as we know it.

Could it be too late for mankind, have we ruined the earth so much that it is now beyond repair?

Only time and the skills of a few amazing people and the help from an unexpected source will tell.

The world as we know it, it seems is in the hands of just one man…

"The Antichrist will be the infernal prince
again for the third time…so many evils shall be
committed by the means of Satan, the infernal
prince, that almost the entire world shall be
found undone and desolate.
Before these events happen, many rare birds
will cry in the air, "Now! Now!" And
sometime later will vanish.

Nostradamus…circa 1550.

"The sun is always shining. We have
oxygen, trees, birds. There's so many good
things on Earth still.
We haven't destroyed everything."

Ziggy Marley…circa 1990.

Table of Contents

Introduction

As with many other native organisms, birds help to maintain population levels of their prey and predator species, and after death, provide food for scavengers and decomposers.

Many birds are extremely important in plant reproduction through their services as pollinators or seed dispersers.

The ecosystem is very finely balanced, many disasters over thousands of years have caused the balance to be tipped.

How many more disasters can 'Mother Earth' handle?

The year is 2057. The Arctic explorer, 'Sir David Matterson' is on its most important mission to date.

The ship is now over 40 years old; however, it is possibly the only ship in the world that is adequate enough for this very important job.

This could be the last chance to save our doomed world.

There have been many 'scaremongers' over the years that are full of 'Doom and Gloom'; however, it's a bit like the old saying, "Cry, Wolf." The problem with that is, that if no one listens to you anymore, then the true consequences could be devastating for everyone.

Could this really be the final nail in Earth's coffin?

Over the past forty years or so, the 'Sir David Matterson' environmental Arctic explorer ship, named after the world-famous filmmaker and world-renowned naturalist, has helped out with thousands of marine and ecological tests and experiments.

The Sir David Matterson had also helped to save the very last remaining whales and dolphins before they were deemed extinct.

It was also involved with the rescue of over five thousand holiday passengers and crew that were onboard the world's largest cruise ship, 'The Millennium Sea Spray'. At the time, it was the largest ship ever built.

'The Sir David Matterson' is sadly now nearing its last days as a sea-worthy ship.

However, hopefully, it will soon be heading for Antarctica, with a selected crew and specially invited experts in their fields, on probably its very last and most important mission.

As soon as a re-fit is done, it will set sail to a secret research centre in Antarctica, with its extremely precious cargo, possibly the very last 'birds' eggs' on Earth.

Another Arctic explorer ship to replace 'The Sir David Materson' is now hurriedly being built; however, at this crucial time, it will not be finished for at least another four years, and sadly, that will probably be too late.

Professor Anthony Denton is regarded as the greatest environmental expert in the world, the famous scientist and ornithologist. He and his team are desperate to reach the research centre in the Antarctic as soon as possible, along with their extremely precious cargo.

Time is of the essence, will they be too late?

The rest of the world is holding its breath.

Along with Professor Denton are Professor Zack Hogan, the world's leading cryogenics expert, Doctor Maria Khan, the world's leading entomologist and Doctor Diane Williams, Professor Denton's protégé.

They are meeting up in Antarctica with Professor James Wilmot, the world-renowned marine biologist.

This could be the very last chance to save the world. Professor Denton fears that it is already 'too late' and that the Earth's birds, fish and many small animals will soon become extinct.

The results of this would be unimaginable.

This would possibly be the last nail in Earth's coffin, as birds and fish are a vital part of the planet's ecosystem.

The survival of the earth could be in the hands of just one man.

I am Professor Anthony Denton. This is my account of the worst disaster that the world has ever seen.

Chapter One
Man's Greed

Over the past 200 plus years, mankind has done its best to destroy our wonderful planet.

Sometimes through ignorance, sometimes through greed and sometimes, it is the aftermath of the previous reasons that have caused the most damage.

Next year, in 2054, there is to be a summit of world leaders. The summit is going to be held in Kyoto, Japan.

This will probably be the most important world summit that has ever been held.

I have also been invited along to give my account of the state of our earth.

On the agenda is my last-ditch plan: 'Protecting, and saving our planet'.

I have been waiting for a very long time for this opportunity to demand that all the world leaders must act now if we are to have any chance to save the planet.

It's a fact, for over the past 100 years or so, the earth's resources have been severely depleted, and mankind has not replaced anywhere near enough to replenish them.

It all probably began back in the 1950s, with the start of the deforestation of most of the world's rainforests, the invention of 'non-reusable' plastic; the 2000s followed with the results of the 'non-reusable' plastic pollution worldwide. Ironically, plastic non-reusable bags were invented in the 1970s, as a way to help with deforestation. Sadly, this plastic alone very nearly wiped out most of the fish and other sea creatures from all of the oceans and seas.

It was estimated that every single fish, shellfish or mammal in the seas and oceans have tiny, so-called, 'microplastics' in their guts.

It was also suggested that back in the 2020s, the 'microplastics' amounted to over 50 trillion particles in the seas and the oceans; that's over 500 times more in number than there are stars in the milky way.

That fact alone is quite shocking.

The palm oil crisis followed soon after, with over 40 million hectares of forests and human habitations destroyed, as the use of palm oil was in massive demand by more and more manufacturers.

Also, there were severe forest fires in the few forests that were left, mainly in North America and Australia, but it was worldwide, and they very nearly finished off the rest of the remaining forests.

It seems that the trees on Earth have had a very hard time with all sorts of things trying to destroy them.

Also, sadly, the number of bees from all around the world was declining at an alarming rate.

This alone would be unimaginable if they disappeared altogether.

There was also that terrible 'nuclear' power plant which exploded in Turkey, in the year 2028; it made an area of 173,000 square miles uninhabitable for supposedly the next 800 years, which cost the lives of over 30,000 people and countless animals.

This terrible explosion also affected parts of Azerbaijan and Georgia, and even the northern part of Iraq.

This was soon after a terrible coronavirus pandemic which lasted for five years or so and cost the lives of over five million people.

Also, in the late 2020s, China and India's air pollution crisis came to a head, and many citizens had to leave for respiratory health reasons.

China has only recently allowed some families to return in the hope of resurrecting the country.

The world weather has also changed dramatically over the past 50 years, with severe flooding, heatwaves and unprecedented changes worldwide.

In the years 2019 to 2025, Australia suffered each year from droughts and terrible bushfires that very nearly wiped out the continent altogether.

Even the 'Dead Sea' has now completely dried up, and the once beautiful city of 'Venice' is no more, as it, too, has sadly been lost to the sea.

In the year 2029, the Bahamas, after suffering the worst hurricanes ever recorded for five years running, were eventually mostly wiped off the world map with the mother of all hurricanes and earthquakes, followed by a massive tsunami, the biggest ever recorded, which resulted in the loss of over 20,000 lives and the total destruction of most of those wonderful islands and its people.

This also affected the south coast of America.

The state of Florida virtually turned into swampland as did California, Arizona and New Mexico.

It was also about this time in 2029 that a massive iceberg which was about 30% of the whole ice-shelf, separated from the main ice-shelf in Antarctica.

This caused the seas to rise by as much as a terrifying five feet, which inevitably caused severe flooding around the world, and it destroyed many coastal towns and cities.

In Antarctica, in the 2020s, most of the ice and snow turned bright red.

It was quite alarming; however, it was caused by red-pigment algae called Chlamydomonas nivalis, which thrives in freezing water as the ice melts during Antarctica's ever-increasing temperatures.

Soon after, there were recordings of unbelievable earthquakes in Antarctica that measured 9.8 on the Richter scale, the largest ever recorded there since 1982, when the first-ever earthquake was recorded there.

Scientists around the world were very concerned about the earthquakes, as they were not sure what that would do to this very fragile environment and to the rest of the world.

This is about the time when the renowned geologist, Professor James Wilmot, and a team of experts were sent out to Antarctica to set up a 'state-of-the-art' laboratory to monitor any future events, as Antarctica seemed to be doomed.

Great Britain and Ireland also had six continuous years of terrible flooding, which caused massive damage to properties, and the loss of many human and animal lives, followed by blazing heat waves during the summers of 2022-29, with record-breaking temperatures reaching an astonishing 53.5 degrees Celsius. This caused massive grass and forest fires, and that led to very poor yields for farmers, followed by four years of the worst flooding ever recorded.

Could things get any worse?

The ozone layer is now estimated to be less than half of what it was in the 1950s and is still shrinking.

There were also the worst droughts in Eastern Europe in living memory in the years of 2022/2024 when many thousands of lives were sadly lost.

In North America and Canada, there were extremely heavy snowfalls in most places. This lasted a whole year and covered the ground from the north to the south. As one leading ecologist put it:

"The world is being crippled."

On the remote islands of 'Galapagos', there was a massive earthquake about 100 miles offshore.

This resulted in a huge tsunami which more or less covered the whole of the islands and washed away many native species of animals and birds.

Only time will tell if this wonderful island group will survive.

Ever since most countries around the world banned the use of petrol or diesel transport, pollution has actually decreased considerably.

Even some aeroplanes and ships have been converted to 'dual-fuel' and the use of solar power has made a great difference.

Greenpeace, as usual, has been very active over the years, working tirelessly trying to convince the world leaders exactly what was going on with the slow but increasing destruction of our beautiful planet.

But sadly, it has always been the greedy international companies and governments that have ignored all the warning signs just for the sake of profit.

One 'so-called' expert came up with the ridiculous theory that all the world's weather problems might have something to do with the astronauts, returning from their trips to Mars; however, that was just another case of 'scaremongering'.

Now, many experts fear that it is 'too late'.

Space travel had never been more important, as it looked like this world was now 'Giving up'.

At the 'Elon Musk' space centre in Florida, they were working on building massive portable buildings that would eventually be taken to Mars, for the use of human habitation.

The first 500 settlers have been chosen, and they are now preparing themselves for their new homes on the red planet.

Meanwhile, on a very remote, tiny island on the far side of the Earth, Supun and his wife, Hiruni, are living a life completely oblivious to the rest of the outside world's events.

They too have suffered from severe weather changes, but they just accept that it's how it's meant to be.

Life on these remote islands has been exactly the same for many hundreds of years, although the technology was never far away from these islands.

The native inhabitants were very reluctant to move along with the times; they were extremely happy with life as they knew it, so why should they change?

They say that, "Why should we comply with modern times when we are perfectly happy as we are?

We have lived the same way for many thousands of years."

Who could argue with that?

Professor Anthony Stephen Denton is not only renowned as one of the world's leading experts on climate change, but he is also one of the world's leading ornithologists.

He has also represented Great Britain at the world summit held in South Africa in the year 2029.

Professor Denton was born into a wealthy academic family. He has two younger brothers, Michael and David, who are both eminent doctors living abroad. He also has one sister, Francis, who is a well-known novelist.

Professor Denton's parents were both very well educated.

His father, Edward, was a lecturer at Cambridge University. He lectured in physics, while his mother, Vivien, held a very important post in the British government.

Edward Denton was also a government advisor, and he was called to advise the prime minister on many occasions.

Life was good for the Denton family; however, they were not shy of work and they all dedicated their lives to their chosen professions.

Professor Denton had been tutored by his late father at Cambridge, where he achieved the highest results possible in biology and geology.

Professor Denton then went on to tutor at Stanford University.

He has been very passionate about the state of the Earth for many years.

He has worked tirelessly along with his late wife, Joanne, trying to get through to the world leaders that if they don't act soon, then sadly, the world as we know it would be doomed. His cries have usually had no effect at all.

Professor Denton is a tall slender man. He has been on many satellite TV and hologram debate shows, discussing his expertise on climate change and his concerns for the world's bird population.

He is very popular with the general public; however, he is not so popular with the politicians and the capitalists of the world.

He is now in his early 70s and this will be his very last mission.

//

This is Professor Denton's dramatic account of the next five extremely important years for our fragile planet.

For many years now, there have been reports that the number of birds, which usually visit Great Britain and all over Europe, seemed to be rapidly declining.

My team and I have done many studies in Britain, Europe and also many places around the rest of the world.

Thousands and thousands of seabirds were the first to be dying off for some strange reason, which no one has been able to explain yet.

Many tests and autopsies have been performed, but up to now, there is absolutely no reason why they should all be dying off; it was a complete mystery.

My team and I have asked for weekly reports from around the world of any unusual bird activity, such as the decline in species, lack of migration, along with the declining numbers.

After a lengthy five-year study, we were convinced that there was a serious problem and that the world's birds were indeed disappearing.

Many specialists also agreed with our findings.

Although the food sources had depleted somewhat around the world, due to various climate change problems, there should still be plenty of food available for the birds to eat.

So why should they be disappearing?

Something had to be done as soon as possible.

As I have said, my team and I have been working tirelessly all over the world for the past few years, and I am extremely worried about the situation.

I have personally reported to the world leaders on many occasions, regarding my fears for the birds and other endangered species of the world.

The birds are slowly declining, and it appears this is for no apparent reason. My team and I are desperate to find out exactly what is causing this terrible tragedy. Other scientists too have been looking at the problem of the declining bird population without any plausible answers.

Also, there seems to be a problem, as many fish from the seas, oceans, rivers and deep lakes are dying in massive numbers.

Although they are ingesting more and more 'microplastics', we don't know if that could be a possibility.

We have done extensive studies on pesticides and various chemicals and fertilisers from around the world, but we have not linked any specific reason why the birds and some small animals and insects are dying off at an alarming rate.

As far back as the year 2015, I was one of the first people ever to report on the terrible plastic pollution problem in the oceans and seas. That major catastrophe took over 30 years before any significant notice was taken, at a cost of about a third of all the fish and sea creatures worldwide.

My main concerns were as I once said, and I quote:

"The biggest threat to mankind since the nuclear bomb."

I have also long been regarded as one of the world's leading experts on environmental and climate change issues, along with the amazing Dutch Professor, Dr Julia Anderson, who is now in her late 40s.

Dr Julia Anderson has fought so hard over the years and she has dedicated her life ever since she was a young teenager back in 2018, when she single-handedly started to protest at her university to get the world to listen to her concerns about the world's environmental problems.

This one protest led to the rest of the world's students striking for one day each month, to protest about what was happening to the world and to try and convince governments and world leaders that they must act 'NOW' before it is too late to change the world for our children's future.

Julia was also responsible for getting many changes throughout the world, although she was ridiculed and ignored by many governments and world industrialists.

Dr Anderson is the youngest ever recipient to be given 'The Nobel Prize in Physics' for her amazing work.

Professor Denton and his love of birds is world-renowned. He has written over twenty books in his earlier years and they are still highly regarded as the Bibles for birds.

He and his late wife, Joanne, were both very passionate about the survival of the wildlife of the world, especially birds.

Professor Denton was regarded by many as the greatest scientist since the late Professor 'Stephen Hawking'.

Professor Denton's late father, Edward, was also a leading scientist and staunch environmentalist.

He too was very passionate about the survival of the Earth; however, he was sadly killed on an expedition trying to find a solution for the palm oil crisis back in the year 2020.

At the time, there was speculation Professor Denton's father's death was not an accident; however, nothing could be proved.

Professor Denton still has his doubts.

So far my extensive findings of the birds and fish disappearances have fallen on deaf ears, and it was now time for me to make a passionate last stand at the world summit.

The world summit meetings have now become completely different from those in the past.

Nowadays, there are only about 50 people who actually attend in person, while the remaining world leaders attend via electronic screens and holographic images.

I have insisted on being there in person, and I will not leave until I get an 'entire world' response regarding my findings. It's now a matter of life or death.

I have never been more passionate about anything before in my life.

The summit was well into its fifth day before I was allowed to read my report.

It told of my findings regarding the bird and the fish population disappearing worldwide and for concerns that if nothing is done soon, we could lose thousands and thousands of species of birds and some animals and insects, if not all of them. So many are being lost each year and we cannot find why.

Many of the dead birds have been examined, yet no one has come up with an answer.

If it continues at this rate, this would lead to devastating effects all over the world. We do not know what would happen to the world's vegetation.

It was a very passionate and heartfelt speech that left me totally exhausted.

Sadly, as usual, the response was 'lukewarm' to say the very least.

Firstly, as usual, most of the world leaders blamed each other for the problems. Secondly, Russia and China denied that there even was a problem, and they blatantly refused to accept my report, even though Russia had suffered from another terrible pandemic in 2028, which eventually cost the lives of over two million people worldwide.

Thirdly, America even suggested that according to another report, everything in the world was normal. Apart from the extreme weather conditions that everyone was experiencing, there was absolutely no need to worry; it was just nature taking its course.

I was absolutely outraged; I set out to prove them all wrong.

I made passionate speeches at Cambridge, Oxford and The Harvard universities, demanding immediate change.

I even made a holographic video which I managed to have shown on various satellite television stations.

The response from the general public was amazing: students from all over Europe and various countries organised demonstrations, and they also partitioned parliament.

Even the newly built New York 'White House Tower' had daily demonstrations outside; sadly, nothing significant changed, and life just went on as usual.

Why could they not see what was happening?

Some things had changed, but sadly the animals were neglected and many species continued to die out or become extinct altogether.

Unfortunately, the wonderful orangutans were now down to just four pairs worldwide. Tigers, giraffes and even the wonderful common honeybees from all around the world were now almost extinct.

Many species of animals and insects are at severe risk; even crocodiles, the oldest known reptiles on earth, are now on the danger list.

Professor Denton's late wife Joanne had made it her mission, and she had worked extremely hard for many years trying to save the last crocodiles. However, it was on one such trip to Africa on a special crocodile reserve that a young student had accidentally left a security door open in a confined enclosure for the crocodiles. Professor Joanne Denton at the time was examining a sedated crocodile when another crocodile escaped through the open door.

Unfortunately, it crept up behind her; she did not stand a chance.

Sadly, she lost her life. It was a terrible accident and everyone was devastated, especially the young student.

She died doing what she was very passionate about.

I was now at my wit's end trying to get the world leaders to agree to protect the earth before it was too late.

One Russian 'oligarch' was even said to be trying to build a 'Huge Ark' somewhere in Russia.

He intended to collect as many endangered species of animals as possible.

However, due to many protests from all around the world, he was stopped from building it before it got off the ground, as all he really wanted to do was to make even more money from suffering animals.

Meanwhile, back at the other end of the world:

Supun and his wife, Hiruni, live on a remote island in the 'Cocos Keeling islands', a very remote group of islands that are situated between Australia and Sri-Lanka.

Supun and Hiruni are the only inhabitants on one of the tiny islands in the group of about 27 islands, where only two islands are actually inhabited.

Supun and Hiruni both decided about twenty years earlier, to move onto one of the smallest uninhabited islands.

They named it 'Rumah', which means 'home' in their language.

They had a son named 'Calhua' however, one terrible night, they had a very severe tropical storm, and sadly, Calhua was washed into the raging sea; he was never seen again.

Supun and Hiruni both then decided that they would stay on the island and set up their home as this is where the spirit of Calhua is.

Supun and Hiruni are completely self-sufficient; they catch all their food from the sea and they manage to grow a few vegetables.

They just like to be alone, with no contact from the outside world.

Chapter Two
Decline

The year is now 2054, and there have been reports of unusually huge swarms of insects in and around the South African bush.

At first, people thought that they were swarms of locusts on the move, but after a group of rangers were out protecting the last surviving giraffes (sadly, the elephants and rhinos are nearly all extinct), they saw one of the huge swarms for themselves.

A ranger sent this report back to the authorities:

As we approached the area in the bush, suddenly the sky turned black. As we looked up, we saw a massive cloud of insects; it must have been about half a mile across, and the noise was immense.

We had to run, and we locked ourselves inside our trucks to protect ourselves; however, somehow the flies still managed to get inside the trucks. We were all soon covered with thousands of the black flies; unfortunately, one of our rangers died of asphyxiation, as the flies managed to find a way inside his mask and they ended up in his nose and his mouth.

The flies were choking him. We tried our best to help him but there were too many flies; it was a horrible sight to see.

Eventually, we tried to start our solar-powered electric truck, but there was a huge flash of sparks from the batteries due to them being covered with the flies. We covered our mouths with handkerchiefs and put our hands over our eyes and ears; it was like something out of a horror film!

Eventually, after what seemed like an eternity, but actually it was about half an hour or so, the flies moved on; somehow, the rest of us managed to survive although a couple of us had some difficulty breathing at times.

We eventually managed to start up the trucks and made our escape; we were all extremely shaken.

When I read his report, I was absolutely at my wit's end.

The loss of life while trying to save our planet was devastating.

Many people have, over the years, sadly lost their lives whilst trying to save our planet; however, it still hurts every time it happens.

My team and I met up back at my office, where we decided that we must go out to South Africa, to see for ourselves exactly what was going on.

We gathered some special safety equipment, and we headed straight to South Africa to investigate.

There had been warnings to air traffic that many swarms of flies had been clogging up some of the light aircraft; however, we were going out on an RAF cargo plane and we were assured that the plane would be fine.

When we arrived safely, we were greeted by two rangers that worked at the lodge and were in the party of rangers that went to the bush on that fateful day.

Once we arrived at the lodge, we loaded up some solar-powered trucks, which the government had supplied for us, with our essential supplies and equipment.

We then set off towards the area from where that terrible report had come, regarding the swarm of flies.

When we set off to the bush, we could not believe what we saw.

There were dead animals everywhere, even large animals such as elephants, giraffes and we even saw a dead rhinoceros.

Eventually, we arrived in the area where the rangers had had that terrible attack. Straight away, we noticed a strange 'eerie' atmosphere all around.

We then drove our solar-powered electric trucks to the edge of the bush; however, we were all in for quite a shock.

Stopping at a lookout post, myself and one of my colleagues climbed up onto a truck to view the surroundings. In the distance, I could see many masses of black murmurations of what at first, looked just like starlings or birds of some kind, but as I zoomed in closer, I soon realised that they were not birds at all but massive swarms of black flies, just as the rangers had reported.

I dropped my binoculars down to my waist, and I stood there stunned at what I had seen. I then turned to my colleagues and I said,

"This looks exactly like what I have been warning everyone about. I cannot see or hear any birds or living animals anywhere. We must put on our protective clothing and investigate further."

My team and I discussed how we would investigate. We decided, after reading the report from the rangers, that we would take the trucks away from the bush; we would then cover the trucks up as best as we could and walk the remainder of the journey.

The arrangements were made, and we set up camp for the night as we wanted to get an early start the very next day.

Morning arrived, and after a very restless sleep, once we were dressed into our protective clothing, we set off on foot into the bush.

There was a real sense of anticipation amongst my team, mainly due to the loss of one of the rangers from the previous trip to the bush.

As we approached the bush, even though we had special respirators on, we could still smell death everywhere. On the ground all around us, lay hundreds of skeletons of birds and a few small animals. Some animals were in a state of decay, and some were as if they had just died; they were all covered in thousands and thousands of the black flies, so much so that it was difficult to tell exactly what the animals were.

There was a horrible continuous buzzing noise everywhere, yet also an eerie silence; it was very disturbing.

Our guide stopped, he then pointed up into the top of some trees.

We all looked up into the tree canopy that he was pointing at.

What, at first, looked like foliage of leaves in the tree, on closer inspection, we soon realised that it was massive swarms of flies; it was a horrible sight.

Suddenly, one of the swarms of flies took flight, and it was heading straight towards us.

We all quickly dropped to the ground, waiting to be smothered by the flies, but amazingly, the swarm flew just above our heads and off into the distance. The noise was horrendous; it was very frightening.

Once the flies had gone, we all stood up and I gestured to my colleagues to follow me.

We then made our way slowly through the bush. We were shocked at the number of carcasses that lay all around; the stench of rotting flesh was everywhere.

After taking many photographs and videos, I had seen enough.

Before we returned to the camp, I ordered my colleagues to collect as many varieties of the dead birds and small animals as possible and to pack them into some vacuumed containers that we had brought with us, so that we could examine them back at the laboratory.

Finally, when we had seen enough, we decided to return to the trucks, my team did not need asking twice.

When we eventually got back to the trucks, they were covered all over in masses of flies.

My first thought was why would they cover our trucks?

Surely, they could not eat them.

My team managed to brush most of the flies away, and we then realised that inside the truck was a metal sandwich box that had been torn apart. We thought that flies must have been after its contents. Why when there was rotting flesh all around was quite baffling. We did not know how the flies had managed to enter the cab.

I had filmed the whole expedition on my head camera.

It took us an hour to clear away all the flies and to start up the trucks.

Once we had returned safely back at base camp, we played back the recording.

Having watched it, we came to the conclusion that all the birds, even the vultures, had all died for a reason not yet known to us, which was why the flies were in such numbers.

The vultures and crows were not there to clean away the rotting flesh, hyenas or any other carrion-eating animals were also nowhere to be seen.

I immediately sent a copy of my film to all the heads of governments across the world. I also demanded a meeting as soon as possible, as this could be the start of the worst epidemic that the world had ever seen.

At about the same time that I was preparing my report of our trip to South Africa, I received yet another report; this time it was from India, regarding massive swarms of mosquitoes invading villages.

"Perhaps we are already too late," said one of my team members.

Back at my laboratory, my team had started to dissect some of the birds that we had brought back from South Africa, hoping that we could find something out of the ordinary.

As one of my team was just about to pack up for the evening, he saw something unusual.

What my colleagues eventually found was quite shocking.

Test after test, he could not see anything unusual. However, under a very powerful electro microscope, he saw something that he had not noticed before.

There was just one very tiny dead red worm inside the stomach intestine of the bird. It was so tiny in fact that without the microscope, it was not properly visible. It was about the size of half a grain of rice, he could barely see it. It was a red 'maggot-like' worm, which he could not identify.

He then checked another bird for the worm, just in case it was a one-off, and, yes, there it was, he checked another just to confirm, yes another tiny worm.

Once he knew what to look for, he found it easy to see.

Could this be at last the breakthrough that we had been looking for? We really needed a break.

I then ordered the rest of my team to examine some of the dead fish for the worms. I had told them exactly where and what to look for, and after some microscopic viewing, they also found the red worms inside the fish intestines.

I immediately sent for one of my former colleagues to help us out. She is the leading expert in bacteria and infectious diseases, Doctor Maria Khan.

She was very eager to help us and she immediately dropped everything and boarded a plane to London.

Dr Maria Khan had been a part of the team that had found a cure for the terrible infectious disease outbreak in India in 2026-28; the disease led to over 108,000 human deaths.

Also, she helped to find an antidote for the coronavirus in the early 2020s.

She too was also highly regarded by her peers in the scientific world.

Dr Khan is married to Dean Khan; he is an astronaut. He was the very first astronaut to spend over two years continually in a space station, preparing for the first manned trip to Mars.

Professor Denton and Doctor Khan had worked alongside Joanne Denton on various occasions, they had all worked well together, and they were all as passionate as each other about their work.

Dr Khan and Joanne Denton were the best of friends at university.

It was Dr Khan and her husband, Dean, who introduced Joanne to Professor Denton at a convention on climate change back in the 2020s.

After a whirlwind romance and a lavish wedding, they all went out to South America, on a trek through the Amazon instead of Professor Denton and Joanne going on a honeymoon.

A meeting with the world leaders was set for one week's time at the 'Stephen Hawking Building' in London.

Meanwhile, a team of scientists was sent out to India to investigate the ever-growing mosquito plague.

Sadly, it seemed to be the same problem as the flies that were in South Africa; however, this time, there were massive swarms of mosquitoes, not flies, and they are probably a bigger threat to humanity than flies.

By now, the worldwide cases of malaria had increased by over a staggering 200%.

Dr Khan had ordered the production of 'chloroquine and quinine sulphate' (ATCs) to be increased worldwide to help to treat malaria sufferers.

Sadly, this was to prove a very difficult task, as the 'cinchona tree', from where quinine is produced, was one of the trees that had suffered badly from deforestation in South America.

Reports were now coming in from as far away as Australia, China and South America that there were massive swarms of locusts and flies and they were absolutely unstoppable.

The world now could not keep up with the massive demand for safe insecticides.

One of the most devastating things to happen regarding this terrible problem was that bees from all over the world were being destroyed by the masses of flies and locusts.

For many years, the bee population has been declining worldwide. Many steps have been taken over the past fifty-odd years, ever since the problem was realised.

There were over 20,000 different species of bees around the world.

If they were to totally disappear, then this would be devastating to many plants and flowers which depend on bees pollinating them.

The birdlife had now almost completely disappeared from all around the world, just as Professor Denton had been predicting for the past few years.

All the crops and vegetation everywhere were being destroyed at an alarming rate, planes could not spray the crops as the insects were clogging up their engines, even if they could get the insecticides.

Even the solar-powered planes were of no use because the swarms of flies covered the solar panels and that deemed them useless.

Someone must come up with a solution, and soon, before the whole world is starved to death.

One of my greatest concerns was for 'drinking water'.

Over the past thirty years or so, drinking water has decreased worldwide.

I know that this sounds ridiculous and far-fetched. However, due to many environmental reasons, coupled with the ever-increasing planet population, many scientists like me believe that drinking water has decreased by as much as 40% over the past fifty years or so, and that's worldwide, not in just very hot countries.

The situation is now getting critical as many freshwater processing plants are also having great difficulty providing enough fresh water, due to the insects clogging up the machinery.

The world's leading scientists and inventors were very busy working on plans to help.

By now, it is a race against time, and the time is running out very fast.

Chapter Three
Crisis Points

All around the world, there are now reports of birds and fish dying in Biblical numbers.

Sadly, even penguins were dying in some of the coldest regions of the world, however, this could be down to the fish supply also dying off.

At the meeting in London of the world leaders, I could at last gave a report on the finding of the tiny red worms found in the birds and the fish.

After some embarrassing pats on my back and congratulations, my team and I were given the job of trying to find out exactly what was causing this worldwide epidemic.

We had already been working tirelessly on a plan to try to stop this terrible situation.

At the meeting, I told the world leaders exactly what my plan was and that we had taken the decision that my team would travel the world to collect as many birds' eggs as they could, with the help of many teams from around the world, before the rest of the birds had disappeared completely.

This task was going to be a massive undertaking as there are (or were) over ten thousand different types of species of birds around the world.

America, up to now, had been strangely reluctant to help, as, for some strange reason, the birds in North America seemed to not be affected as much as the rest of the birds around the world, although there were many bird and fish deaths.

However, my team and I went out to America to collect the eggs just the same.

Everyone was, at last, seemed to be waking up to the crisis that I had been warning them about for the past few years.

The biggest problem was, what exactly was causing this terrible bird and fish epidemic?

Was it the tiny red worm that was found in each of the dead birds and also in the fish intestines, if so, how were they killing them? They had still not yet been identified, and as the worms were dead inside them, it made it even more difficult to identify them.

The DNA from the worms, which were extremely difficult to collect, did not match anything on record.

Thousands and thousands of dead birds were also being washed up onto shores all over the world; it was horrific.

Many top scientists from all countries around the world were now working on trying to solve this mystery of the birds dying.

It was concluded that the tiny worms were incubating inside the intestines of birds and fish, and it was this that was causing them to die, but the strange thing was that the worms never actually developed into anything further.

Were they really responsible for the deaths? It seemed like the worms were poisoning them from inside their intestines and then both the host and the worms died.

Why? Where have they suddenly come from? although I think that they may have been here for many years and we simply did not know.

We must find out before it is too late.

I even doubted myself that the worms were the reason for the deaths. If I was wrong, then it would be much too late now to find out the real reason for this epidemic because no one else had come up with any other reason.

The one good thing to come out of this very worrying time was that most of the world's religions had decided to put their differences behind them and that they would all work together as one.

It was an amazing thing to see.

By now, the malaria epidemic in India and elsewhere around the world was now out of control. Mosquito nets were of no use whatsoever, due to the size of the multiple swarms, sadly, there was nowhere to hide.

During this infestation of mosquitoes, my youngest son David, contracted malaria while he was working out in India, helping the doctors out there to try to control this terrible infestation.

After a couple of months, sadly David passed away.

This made me more and more determined to solve the problem.

The swarms were travelling around India at an alarming rate, and they were threatening many neighbouring countries.

Most of Europe, Asia and Russia were now having the swarms of flies and mosquitoes, and rivers and seas full of dead rotting fish.

Thousands upon thousands of children and adults were inoculated against malaria, however, the inoculations did not seem to make much difference, as malaria seemed to be spreading everywhere and any treatment was very difficult to get.

Ever since the early 2000s, and before, more and more people have become vegetarians or vegans this is a good thing, as this alone has helped to reduce many health and environmental problems.

Because more and more people have turned to vegetarianism, this increased demand for bean-based foods over the past fifty-odd years. Many farmers have converted from livestock farming to soya bean and other beans' farming.

In North America alone, over 70% of farms now produce thousands and thousands of tonnes of soya beans, which are distributed worldwide.

Also, lentils, chickpeas, quinoa and hemp production has increased by over 80% in the past fifty years.

Sadly, many, many thousands of fields full of these beans worldwide were being destroyed by the swarms of locusts.

This is obviously of great concern, as many people rely on this form of cheap food.

This is just another problem that the world is facing.

Now, as if things could not get any worse, there was yet another world problem: 'Rats'.

We all knew that it is virtually impossible to get rid of rats.

This insect epidemic was getting out of hand, so too were rats.

There were plagues of rats nearly everywhere, especially if a swarm of mosquitoes or flies were around.

Some people welcomed the rats, as they said that they were actually helping to get rid of the flies and the mosquitoes.

But mainly, people were very afraid of the rat infestations everywhere.

Many people were too afraid to go outside for fear of being attacked and bitten by them.

'Leptospirosis', commonly known as 'Weil's disease', caused by rats, was spreading everywhere, mainly in children who were playing outside. There were many deaths due to this nasty disease.

However, in some countries, the rats were actually welcomed as food.

Many parts of India, and also China, had been known to eat rats, even before this infestation, so they were pleased to see so many.

Who knows, we may all have to eat rats if we cannot resolve the climate situation.

Soon, there were reports from America that more and more of their birds had been found dead, including bald eagles, along with thousands of salmon in Canada.

This produced a quick response from *President Sandra Hopwood*.

The Americans have, at last, suddenly became interested in the world epidemic.

President Sandra Hopwood is America's first female president. She is a very powerful and driven woman; she was well educated at Harvard University where she excelled.

President Hopwood's late father, Theodore, (named after the late Theodore Roosevelt) had also served as president ten years earlier. He was also a very powerful force.

He and Sandra had many 'heated discussions' over the years, and it usually ended up with them agreeing not to agree.

Sadly, it was his power crazy stance that eventually led to his assassination.

President Hopwood is now forty years old; she has been married to Hellen for ten years, they have two children, Grace and Danny.

Ms Hopwood also has no time for hanger-ons or indeed anyone trying to gain favour with her.

She definitely inherited that from her late father. President Hopwood is not a traditionalist at all; she is very much her own boss.

President Hopwood's wife, Hellen, is also a politician, she holds the post of defence secretary.

One of the very first things that President Hopwood did when she was in office was to relocate from the 'White House' in Washington into a brand new modern tower block building in 'New York', which she and Hellen named 'The White House Tower'.

"I want to be accessible to all the citizens of America," she once stated in a news conference.

Also, she did not agree with an inscription that is on a marble fireplace in the old 'White House' in Washington, which was put there by the late President Franklin Delano Roosevelt. The inscription was taken from a quote of a letter written by the late President 'John Adams' that read:

"May none but honest and wise men
ever rule under this house."

President Hopwood did not like this message at all, especially in today's modern society where women hold most of the world's top jobs.

She decided to put up her own plaque in her new office which read...

"A woman's place is certainly <u>not</u> in the home."

President Hopwood had decided, soon after her inauguration, to make a change and move to New York, which was much to the disgust of many of the older generation; however, the young politicians were behind her from the start.

I eventually received a video call directly from President Hopwood, from her new office in New York.

She literally begged me to visit her as soon as possible, in order to bring the Americans up to date with my research.

I politely told the President that if she wanted to meet up with me, then *she* would have to meet *me* in Los Angeles, as I was planning a trip there to meet up with *Professor Zak Hogan* the next month.

President Hopwood agreed, and we set a date for a month's time.

Professor Zak Hogan is regarded as an extremely intelligent man, and also he is the world leader in his field of 'cryogenics' which he has dedicated his life to.

He is now in his 50s; he is often regarded as a 'genius' by many of his colleagues and fellow scientists.

Professor Hogan now lives in Los Angeles, and he is single. He says, "I am married to my work."

He is also heavily involved with the first astronauts that went on the famous first mission to Mars, in the year 2032.

His work on suspended animation was a great success, which allowed the astronauts to be suspended in a 'semi-conscious' state, and then subsequently 'reinstated' them back to normal, from their very long journey to Mars and then back to Earth.

This was regarded as an amazing achievement.

Back in London, King William had recently reported that sadly, all the swans and the other birds at the new 'Queen Elizabeth Palace' had died, even the world famous ravens at the Tower of London had died.

Hyde Park had been cordoned off as a clean-up was in operation. Trafalgar Square too looked deserted without its famous pigeons.

Many thousands of rats also helped with the clean-up.

By now, my teams have collected approximately four thousand different species of birds' eggs from many different countries.

We had decided to leave the fish for now and to just concentrate on collecting the birds' eggs.

However, live birds were becoming increasingly more difficult to find, as the deaths were now rising at an alarming rate.

We did not want to collect live birds as we were concerned that they could possibly contaminate other birds and we did not want to take that risk.

Dr Khan and I held a crisis meeting to decide exactly how to store and keep all the eggs that had been collecting safe.

After hours and hours of discussions, it was decided that we would take the advice from

Professor Zak Hogan, as he had previously developed a way to keep hundreds of different insects and small animals, even humans, in suspended animation with amazing results.

That is why it was decided that he was the person that Professor Denton called to ask if he could help us out.

Professor Hogan was only too willing and very eager to help; he had read all of my reports. In fact, he had already been working tirelessly on keeping the eggs safe. He had also designed a special bubble type ice-wrap, to protect the birds' eggs, and it also helped to keep them at a certain controlled temperature to keep the eggs cool until they arrived at his laboratory.

The very next day, Dr Khan and I boarded a plane to Los Angeles to meet up with Professor Zack Hogan and President Hopwood.

As the plane was nearing 'Trump International Airport', it suddenly started to climb very steeply; we could hear the engines were at full throttle.

The captain warned the passengers to fasten seat belts and 'hold on tight'. Then the plane suddenly went into a steep dive; we were all very concerned hanging onto our seats.

After a short while, the captain announced that there were severe engine problems and that he would have to make an emergency landing at an airport close to 'Trump International Airport'.

The plane's crew prepared everyone for an emergency landing and fortunately, the plane landed safely.

When everyone had disembarked, Professor Denton and Dr Khan asked the captain what had been the problem with the plane. The captain explained,

"As we were approaching Trump Airport, at about twelve thousand feet, we came across what at first I thought was a huge storm cloud straight ahead of us. I saw it on the radar; however, when we got closer, we realised that it was not a storm cloud, but it was a massive swarm of locusts.

I was amazed how high an altitude the swarm was, so I had to take immediate avoiding action. If I had not been quick enough, then both of the engines would have stalled, engulfed by the locusts.

"This is the second time this week that one of our planes has had to make an emergency landing for the same reason. If this continues, then our luck is going to run out."

There had also been recent reports from all around the world about aeroplanes crashing or having to take drastic action in order to land due to massive swarms of flies or locusts, and if it continued, then all aircraft around the world would have to be grounded.

That would be yet another disaster.

This highlighted just one of the hundreds of problems that the world was facing at this critical time.

In Russia, President Volgograd had declared that he would offer a reward of ten million euros to anyone who could find out about the worms and how to stop them.

This offer had caused mayhem, as every so-called or money-making scientist was destroying many of the remaining birds.

Yet again, I pleaded with the world leaders to try to stop any so-called experiments with the dead or live birds, and also anyone offering rewards. I called for a committee to be set up and any future suggestions would have to be discussed and agreed with the experts.

Luckily, they acted fast enough and ordered all non-authorised tests and rewards to be stopped immediately or face a life in prison.

Chapter Four
Professor Denton's Plan

Eventually, myself and Dr Khan reached the laboratory of Professor Zack Hogan, who was patiently waiting for us, along with President Hopwood.

I told them about our ordeal with the aircraft and they understood that it was a serious problem and forgave us for being late.

After formal introductions, Professor Hogan closed his office door, closed the blinds and then we started our very important urgent meeting.

I opened my holographic laptop and I started to explain my proposal:

"Dr Khan and I, along with many of the finest scientists from around the world, have still not yet determined exactly what the worm is or indeed why it has caused such devastation. One theory we have is that after the severe worldwide climate changes, i.e., the heatwaves followed by the severe droughts, earthquakes and floods back in 2051, somehow these tiny worms, that were until recently not known to mankind, must have somehow emerged from the Earth's crust undetected. How and where? We don't yet know. Then they have made their way into the digestive systems of all birds and fish.

"Why birds and fish? We are unsure. What for? We don't know.

"The worms seem to be a completely new species not known to us, but they must poison the birds and fish.

"I will now hand you over to Dr Khan, who will explain."

"Thank you, Professor Denton, It is my firm belief that the worms have been lying 'dormant' for millennia, and due to the various extreme climate conditions, the worms have indeed, somehow, emerged from the Earth's crust, and also from the sea and lake beds. This same thing must also have happened many, many thousands of years ago too, as a leading Egyptologist has recently found an ancient papyrus, apparently written by an Egyptian scientist from circa 3000 BC, where he told of a time when a disease that caused 'The birds of the skies and the fish of the sea' to suddenly disappear or die, without any known reason.

"He went on to say that there was, 'Great famine, due to many swarms of locusts, and the waters disappeared and there were great earthquakes on the lands.'

"At the moment that is where I am up to."

"Thank you, Professor Khan, for your very interesting report, please rest assured that my team of entomologists and I have done extensive tests on the worms.

"It was a revelation when I read that ancient papyrus, but the problem is, that although it sounded exactly the same situation that we are encountering now, he did not give any further details about what happened to stop the worms, or how, or if the birds and fish returned.

"Obviously they did eventually return," said Professor Denton.

"That was very interesting, Dr Khan," said President Hopwood, "Surely you must be onto something with that amazing find?"

"Yes, I agree, but we need to put a stop to what's happening right now. We have a proposal for you, Professor Hogan," said Dr Khan.

"I am only too glad to help you with whatever I can contribute. What exactly is your proposal?"

"After much debating, we think that we need to somehow freeze or suspend all of the birds' eggs that we collect so that one day, we will be able to incubate them in the future.

"Then we should be able to reintroduce the birds back into the environment if the world is not destroyed first!"

Dr Kahn then interjected to explain to President Hopwood that, "This is why we have asked Professor Zak Hogan to come on board; as you know, he is the world's best cryogenics and suspended animation expert.

"I will now hand you over to Professor Hogan at this point."

"Thank you, Doctor Khan, I will now bring you all up to date. At the moment, we have all the eggs, which we have collected so far, in special vacuum packaging in a stable temperature-controlled environment, to try to protect them as much as possible, without damaging them in any way.

"However, it is proving to be a very delicate exercise, and sadly, we have had a few eggs that have been accidentally broken."

"Your proposal sounds like a good one, Professor Hogan, thank you.

I don't see any reason why it would not work, but it would have to be done in a very isolated place where there is absolutely no chance of contamination.

"Therefore, my team has come up with the perfect place to store the eggs: the Antarctic. There is already a secret fully equipped laboratory there and we have been given complete authority to use the facility as we need to. However, I need more specialised equipment to be installed," said Professor Denton.

"Just let me know exactly what equipment you need, Professor Hogan and rest assured that

America will supply it," said President Hopwood.

"Thank you, Madam President, that's a very generous offer.

"I am also delighted to announce that we have been given the 'green light' to use the 'Sir David Matterson' arctic explorer and the crew for our trip to Antarctica."

"Well, it does not get better than that! Very well done, Professor Denton," said Professor Hogan.

"It is going to be a perilous journey by ship, but we dare not risk flying out to Antarctica.

"By now most of the world's shipping has come to a standstill due to the masses of dead birds and fish that are floating in the oceans and seas."

"Our first priority must be to find out where these worms have been and are coming from, and also, how the birds are ingesting them; also, why is it happening and how can we stop them," said Dr Khan.

President Hopwood congratulated them all on doing such a wonderful job so far and she was only too glad to help in any way possible. She said,

"I have many people, only too willing and ready to help you in any way at all, Professor Denton; just say the word and I will arrange it."

"Thank you, President Hopwood, we knew that we could count on you."

After our meeting, I contacted my team of scientists to put them all in the picture, telling them to upscale their collection of eggs, as time was now running out.

India had, by now, been declared a no-go zone for the rest of the world, and there were also concerns that the massive number of locusts were heading north, towards Europe, eating virtually everything that was in sight.

In addition to this, there were also reports of massive swarms of flies that were clogging up the air conditioning units and invading shops and offices if people opened their windows.

The outbreak was now classed as a 'critical' level and it could only get worse unless someone could come up with a solution. The situation looked hopeless.

Meanwhile,

Supun and Hiruni, meanwhile, were completely oblivious to the rest of the world's events; they had built themselves a home and shelter over the years, to protect themselves from the storms and blazing sunshine. They were now both in their 50s yet they were very healthy and happy.

Supun and Hiruni loved wildlife, especially birds.

They both decided that they would like to build an aviary, however, due to the size of the island, they decided to build a floating platform on the sea in a small cove where the birds would be protected. It started quite small at first but over the years, it has grown into quite a substantial size, where they have ended up with a great collection of many exotic birds.

It was amazing how many different species of birds were captured by Supun over the years, he was dedicated to saving as many birds as he could possibly look after.

In one part of India, away from the cities and towns, a group of Apiarists had managed to fence off a huge area, about a five-mile square.

They had been collecting as many bees as they could and they kept them in a safe environment for a year or so, protected from the flies and locusts, with great success.

They then placed the finest nylon netting available all around and above the whole twenty-five square mile area.

They then planted as many species of flower and plant life as they could possibly collect.

Once they were certain that the plants were not in any danger, they placed hundreds of beehives around in the hope of the bees pollinating them.

They monitored the bees both day and night.

So far, the bees were acting normal however, only time will tell.

Chapter Five
Time Is Running Out

The disaster was now escalating at an even more phenomenal rate; it had now been nearly a year since my proposal.

The birds and many other species of animals and insects were continually dying in every country and in all situations. Strangely, even some of the birds that were caged in aviaries were dying, or those kept at homes and zoos, which seemed very strange.

It seemed that all birds and even small animals were not safe anywhere.

Also, many small animals were being attacked by the locusts, flies and now, rats. Something had to be done, and quickly.

Professor Julia Anderson and I were very still actively trying to rally the world leaders into acting faster than they were; it seemed to be working a little.

One of the biggest problems around the world was that even common everyday chickens were dying.

As chickens were one of the main sources of nutrition worldwide, along with eggs and fish, it was causing thousands of people to die of malnutrition.

Over the past year or so, new pesticides and insecticides had been tried out on the flies and mosquitoes, with little success. Some of the insecticides had proved to be lethal, to certain humans as people were dying from asthma and lung diseases due to the crop spraying that had gone into the food chain. Eventually, it was decided that all 'experimental' insecticides were to stop immediately. The world leaders were desperate to know what to do next.

They held a meeting after meeting but to no avail.

Meanwhile, my team had been working tirelessly for over two years and the egg collection operation was so large that they were running out of space to store the vacuumed eggs.

Professor Hogan and his team of experts had also been working tirelessly for a year, supervising the work in the laboratory in Antarctica, and the massive cryogenic chambers were now nearly ready.

The 'Sir David Matterson' Arctic explorer had now been fully re-fitted out, as requested by Professor Denton and Professor Hogan.

It was moored up in Southampton England, and it would soon be heading out to South Africa for the final all important re-fit.

Professor Hogan was invited onboard to look around at the re-fit which had been done so far, he was very impressed. Everything was very high-tech and fitted to an amazing standard. He felt sure that it would be absolutely right for the transportation of our precious cargo.

The date of March the 4th, 2056, had been set for the ship to leave Cape Town with the cargo of birds' eggs.

The human death toll worldwide was now estimated to be approximately 28 million people and was rising daily.

Time was running out if the world was to be saved.

My team of egg collectors will be headed by: *Dr Diane Williams*.

Dr Williams had studied under Professor Denton where she too achieved the highest grades possible in ornithology, at Stanford University where Professor Denton was her tutor. Dr Williams is now in her late 40s, she is married to Doctor James Williams. They have one daughter Jody.

Dr Williams took over from Professor Denton as the head of the university five years ago, after the death of his wife Joanne. She had worked tirelessly over ten years with the professor on many projects.

Dr Williams and Joanne Denton had been the best of friends for many years.

Dr Williams and her team had travelled to the far ends of the Earth, collecting birds' eggs.

Dr Williams had, in the back of her mind, an intention to return to the Moloka'i forest reserve, on an island in Hawaii.

Dr Williams was convinced that when they visited Moloka'i the last time, she was quite sure that she had heard a strange bird call that she did not recognise. However, no one else had heard it. They had searched the area where she thought that the sound had come from, but they could not find any trace of a bird, and they decided to leave.

However, as they were quite close to Moloka'i, they decided that if they don't return now, then they may lose the chance to return later.

Dr Williams contacted Professor Denton to ask his permission to return. He said that if she was absolutely sure that she heard a bird there, then he would give her five days to search.

They returned to Moloka'i, taking all their equipment, and headed for the most remote part of the island, the Moloka'i forest reserve.

For two days, they trekked towards the forest near the mountains but they heard nothing. However, just as they were about to pack up and head back to the ship, suddenly one of the team members was sure that he had heard the faint sound of a squawk that was not familiar to him, he was absolutely convinced that it was definitely a bird.

When he explained to Dr Williams the sound that he had heard, she felt certain that it was the same sound that she had heard previously.

She too was convinced that it was 'definitely' a bird, as up to now, they had not seen or heard any other animals there.

Dr Williams then asked her team for 'complete silence' while they waited and listened; they must have waited for at least half an hour and it was absolutely silent, apart from the flies buzzing around them.

Then, just as they were all about to give up, they all heard a squawk.

Dr Williams grabbed the sound recorder's arm and squeezed it so hard that he screamed out. "Sorry," she said.

Everyone was very excited, and they all agreed that it must have been a bird.

They all wanted to set off to search the area as soon as possible, but they decided that they should wait until the morning to make sure that they had all the correct equipment to take with them. They did not want anything at all to jeopardise this vital task.

Dr Williams reported their findings to me, I was elated and I gave her permission to continue as she saw fit.

The morning could not come soon enough, Dr Williams and her team all said that they had hardly slept at all.

Having packed all the equipment and food away, they set off into the volcanic forested hills.

It was a very hard trek, as the whole area was infested with mosquitoes and flies. It was also a very exhausting and an extremely hot and humid trek, as they were all covered in protective netting and clothing. They were also very tired and were only about halfway there.

At about the same time that the team were on Moloka'i, the first group of scientists with the precious cargo of the birds' eggs had now reached the 'Sir David Matterson' ship, which was now safely docked in Cape Town, they had also managed to load their first precious cargo of birds' eggs onboard.

Time was of the essence as the eggs had to be protected and kept at a precise temperature as soon as possible.

In Antarctica, Professor Wilmot and his team had an amazing breakthrough.

One of the specially built unmanned submersibles was investigating the seabed, some 7,000 feet deep.

As the camera operator was looking at the film that had been taken on its previous journey to the seabed, he noticed something very unusual.

There were what appeared to be some very strange-looking fish or sea creatures, which he had never seen before, and as he looked closer, he noticed that they seemed to be feeding on something, however, he could not see exactly what it was that they were eating.

He reported his find to Professor Wilmot; he too was very excited as he was looking at the video.

"We must investigate this further with that special new camera," he said.

His team soon fitted the new camera to the submersible, as they were very eager to launch it. Sadly, there was at that time, a storm was coming in, and it would be too dangerous to send it down to the seabed.

Now it is a waiting game.

By now, Dr William's team had nearly reached the forest, and she decided to rest the team until the morning and then continue their search at first light.

One of the main problems was that they could not use any air transport, as the flies and bugs would have choked up the engines.

They did take a couple of drones along with them on the trek however, they did not want to take the risk of frightening or harming any birds, and the flies would have probably downed them, so they had decided not to use the drones.

The following morning, the team were very eager to set off.

Dr Williams said that this has to be the last day of the search or all the other eggs that they had collected previously would be at risk.

They reached the edge of the trees where they thought that the sound had come from. Dr Williams then asked for complete silence.

Back in London, members of my team had discovered some fossils in the vaults of the Natural History Museum in London.

They had been searching the storerooms ever since they heard the report about the papyrus.

Boxes of fossils had been stored away, many years ago, as they were more or less deemed as uninteresting. The fossils were among about a thousand species that were classified as 'as yet unknown'.

As one of my team was closely examining one of the bird bone fossils, he eventually saw what he thought was a tiny worm-like creature on it, he was not absolutely sure if it was some sort of a plant, seed or root, or indeed a worm.

When he examined another couple of fossils from the same batch, he found more, and he was now convinced that they were tiny worms very similar to the ones in the birds.

After two more eminent scientists and palaeontologists had examined the fossils carefully under an electron microscope, they all agreed that they looked exactly like the worms that they thought had been destroying all the birds.

They were all very excited at the find, as the worm fossils were so very small, less than the size of a grain of rice.

"Ever likely they never saw them before, they are so tiny," said one of my team members.

Slowly and very quietly, Dr Williams and her team moved through the forest area, although it was teeming with mosquitoes and flies, and the humidity was stifling. They were fully protected by their special clothing; however, it made their job a lot more difficult.

Having reached a clearing, they set up their equipment and waited.

"This is the worst part for me," said Dr Williams.

"It is now a matter of luck," she said.

It must have been over an hour later when all of a sudden, they all heard a faint squawk, then a few seconds later, yet another squawk.

The team all looked at each other with excitement.

After confirming they all thought that it definitely was a bird, they all hugged and shook hands, they did not want to cheer in case they frightened the birds away.

"That is the greatest sound that I have ever heard," whispered Dr Williams.

Now they had to try to find out exactly where the squawk was coming from. This was not going to be as easy as they thought.

One of the camera team had brought along a couple of high-powered, heat-seeking, motion-activated cameras. They were very high-tech pieces of equipment.

He set them up near to where they all thought the sound had come from.

About half an hour later, they all heard another squawk and the special cameras immediately started recording, they swung around silently and zoomed in to where they had picked up the sound and where the squawk was coming from, all within a millisecond.

Alex, the cameraman, then downloaded the camera's findings by remote control to his holographic tablet computer.

Everyone gathered around the screen in a huddle, then, suddenly the tablet flickered. "WOW! Just look at that," whispered Dr Williams.

"What is it?" asked a member of the team.

"Well, it is definitely a bird, but I don't think that I have ever seen one of those birds before in my life, but in the back of my memory bank, it looks a little familiar. I wonder what sort of bird it is," said Dr Williams.

"All I know is that it's the best bird that I have ever seen in my entire life," said Alex.

Back in Antarctica, Professor Wilmot declared that the weather was now safe enough to send down the submersible to the bottom of the ocean to, hopefully, find out just what was going on with those strange feeding fish.

Up on deck, they carefully lowered the submersible into the ice-cold water, at the exact spot that it was lowered previously.

It seemed like an eternity for the submersible to reach its target, the water was remarkably crystal clear, even at those depths.

Slowly the operator eased the sub to the location.

Professor Wilmot let out a "yes, I can see them".

Amazingly, the strange fish did not seem to notice the sub. "Perhaps they have no sight," said the camera operator.

"You are probably right," said the professor.

As they got closer and closer, the new camera picked up something that the previous camera could not.

There was what looked like a long narrow crack in the seabed which was probably caused by that severe earthquake a few years ago.

Just then, the cameraman yelled out, "Look there! Can you see what I can see?"

Meanwhile, at the Natural History Museum, there was an equal amount of excitement, as more fossils from the archives were found, among them was a fossil of some of the worms that were among some fish bones.

An emergency meeting was swiftly arranged with myself and other world leaders and scientists.

At the meeting, one of my team unveiled the fossils.

His theory was, as Dr Williams had previously said, that hundreds of thousands of years ago the same thing must have happened.

The worms had invaded the prehistoric birds and fish and wiped them all out.

How or Why? Probably due to weather conditions just like we are experiencing now.

He did not have all the answers, but to him, this was the best, if not the only theory that he had to offer.

Back on Moloka'i, the video of the bird was downloaded and sent directly to me. I became very excited.

Once I had examined it, I told the team that I would closely examine the images and I would message them with my results as soon as possible.

I too thought in the back of my mind that I had also seen this bird before somewhere; however, I could not remember exactly where.

Back on Moloka'i, Dr Williams and the team agreed that they should try to capture one of the birds and try to keep it alive, once they had received permission from me.

Dr Williams received this message from Professor Denton,

"This is absolutely amazing what you have found in Moloka'i! I have searched the records and I have eventually found out that it is a bird that was thought to be extinct.

It is called a 'Po'ouli', Latin name, 'Melamprosops Phaeosoma', pronounced... Poh-oh-u-lee, meaning blackface.

Amazingly, this bird was only first discovered in the early 1970s in Hawaii; it eats mainly snails and it has not been seen for at least 60 years. Back in the 1980s, there was a severe volcanic eruption on Maui, after which the birds had not been seen, and therefore, they were deemed extinct. These birds really are something special to survive everything that they have and also they seem to be immune to the red worms.

This is a real find, especially as it is a live one.

Congratulations to you and your team, excellent work."

Dr Williams then replied, "We are going to try to capture one of the birds, or hopefully a pair, and hope that they will survive the journey to you, that is if you agree?"

"Absolutely, please, please be extremely careful, as they may be the only birds left on earth that are not affected by the worms. Good luck, the survival of mankind could depend on you, so no pressure!"

"No pressure! I don't know about that, however, we have gone over the scenario many, many times regarding how we could capture a bird, and after many suggestions, we decided to place a massive fine net which we have with us all around the canopy of the nearby trees around the birds' nest.

"Hopefully, this will not affect the birds too much. We can then build a platform in a tree adjacent to the bird's tree, and we have a huge butterfly net that we can use to catch a bird unharmed," answered Dr Williams.

"We all know that the birds are in the safest hands possible. Good luck to you all," I replied.

I had been asked to keep King William informed of their progress throughout their work, and when I reported my latest findings back to him in London, he was elated and he sent my team his very best wishes.

By now, nearly all commercial flights had been grounded due to the swarms of locusts and flies clogging up planes' engines.

Meanwhile,

Supun and Hiruni had recently noticed that some of the birds in their aviaries were acting a little strange as they had stopped singing.

Apart from them not singing, they were acting quite normal.

They were still eating and apart from them not singing, they seemed to be in perfectly good health.

Also, they had noticed many dead fish floating around the islands, which was quite unusual.

Supun and Hiruni could not understand what was happening.

They were very concerned for the birds however, their main concern was the fish, as fish were their main source of nutrition and they were not sure if they had been poisoned.

Chapter Six
A Breakthrough

While all the research and egg collecting had been going on, it seemed like all of the countries over the world were, at last, working together where possible to build large fly-proof buildings and houses.

Past problems with each other seemed to have been temporarily forgotten, and the religious leaders were still working very well together.

Also, chemists from all around the world were developing 'safe' insecticides that were safe to humans and animals, to try to eradicate the plagues of flies, mosquitoes and locusts now with some amazing results.

However, nature, it seemed, was still winning the battle and everyone's way of life had now been turned upside down.

Sadly, deaths from various diseases were increasing everywhere.

"Never forget that we did find a solution to the terrible 'Covid Pandemic' back in the 2020s." said one of my assistants.

It was looking like the end of the world as we know it.

Scientists and health officials from all around the world were working extremely hard together, to try to find meat substitutes with enough nutrition to help to feed the starving millions.

The biggest problem is that most meat substitutes are plant-based, and as most of the planting around the world was being destroyed by the locusts, it was extremely difficult to produce more crops.

President Hopwood said that now it was time to turn to the 'Astronauts that have visited Mars'.

During the recent Mars trips, the boffins at the 'Elon Musk Space Centre' had developed some amazing foods for the astronauts to take along with them to Mars, which did not use plant-based materials.

Although the food was chemical-based, it proved to be highly nutritious and very easy to produce.

At first, people were up in arms about having to eat chemicals. However, as there was not much choice, they soon got used to it.

A company was set up to produce the food, and production was non-stop 24/7.

It was a great success.

Back in Antarctica, Professor Wilmot and his team could not believe their eyes.

As they were zooming in on the strange fish, they managed to see exactly what they were eating. Unbelievably, they were eating the tiny red worms that they have found inside the birds and fish intestines.

"This has got to be the source of the devastation around the world. These red worms have somehow evolved again, and the ocean is distributing them to the fish and to the rivers and oceans. The fish and the birds are somehow eating them and it is killing them all.

"They must have been encased under the ice where they were in a state of suspended life for thousands of years, and after that massive earthquake, they have somehow emerged and come back to life.

"We must try to gather some of the worms so that we can examine living ones, perhaps then we could find an antidote," said Professor Wilmot.

They returned the submersible back onboard the ship, and then they re-fitted it with special containers to gather up some of the worms, and also hopefully, some of the strange fish that seemed to be immune to the worms.

Professor Wilmot video called Professor Denton with his amazing news.

"Hello, Professor Denton, I hope that things are going to plan with you."

"Yes, thank you, Professor Wilmot, so far, so good; however, at this time, Dr Williams and her team are hoping to catch a live po'ouli bird, possibly two, back on Moloka'I, so until I know if she has been successful, I am very nervous."

"Well, Professor, on that note, I have some amazing news for you; are you sitting down?"

"Yes, why do you ask?"

"Well, what I am about to tell you and show you, it's possible that you may very well collapse with excitement."

"Really, please go on; whatever could make me that excited, I am very curious to know."

"I am sending you some footage of our submersible.

What you will see will knock you out, believe me."

Professor Wilmot then sent the video to Professor Denton.

Professor Wilmot watched Professor Denton's face, as he saw the video of the strange fish eating the red worms his mouth was open very wide while he was watching it. He then turned to the video camera and he had a tear in his eye.

"I have seen it, but I don't believe it. This is the biggest breakthrough ever, surely, now we can now solve this terrible problem."

"I have even better news for you, Professor; you see, as we are speaking, my team is capturing some of the live worms, and hopefully, some of those strange fish."

"Well, well, well, you have certainly come up trumps this time, Professor Wilmot, I have never been so excited. As soon as you have any more information, please contact me, day or night, and I will arrange to come down to visit you very soon."

"I certainly will, Professor, goodbye."

Back on Moloka'i, Dr Williams and her team were planning when the best time would be to capture one of the birds, or preferably two, a male and a female *po'ouli* bird, if at all possible.

It was not going to be easy, and time was now running out fast.

They had studied the birds very carefully with the remote-controlled cameras, and they had decided that it would be best to try to capture one at night, as then they would be quite docile, they did not want to frighten them in any way.

They found out exactly where the nest was, then they erected the huge very fine net, which covered a very large area above the canopy of the trees so that it did not stop the birds from flying away to gather food.

They wanted to make sure that if they did fly away, then they would eventually only reach the fine net which would not harm them in any way.

It was hoped that the net did not affect the birds.

"It is now or never," said Dr Williams.

Very quietly, they set the trap as soon as they knew that the birds were quietly nesting.

When it was dark enough, they set up the platform on an adjacent tree and waited for the right moment.

It was a very nervous time for the team, but it had to be done just right as they may only get this one chance.

They all had night-vision cameras and headgear.

All of the team members were very quiet as they all knew that what they were about to attempt could go disastrously wrong, and if so, they would probably never get a second chance.

Back in London, my team and I were making good progress.

I had invited the world's best entomologists, palaeontologists and also the best ornithologists to help.

First of all, I showed them the incredible footage that was sent from Professor Wilmot, and as I expected, they were all astonished by it.

I had also recently received a new video message from Antarctica from Professor Wilmot, showing that he had indeed managed to capture many of the red worms and even some of the strange fish. It was quite an amazing achievement that they survived as we all agreed.

My team has also all worked tirelessly day and night studying the fossils.

I personally took on the job of trying to find out everything that was known about the *po'ouli* bird, which was not a great deal.

Apparently, many years ago, after a volcano had erupted on Maui, an island off Hawaii, it had caused massive destruction on the island, and many birds and other animals were destroyed.

The local people had feared that the *po'ouli* birds too had perished. However, they turned out to be very resilient birds and amazingly, the birds had survived; unfortunately, since the early 2000s they had not been seen again.

They were a bit of a phenomenon, as the birds were only discovered in the 1970s and then disappeared not long after.

In the year of 2018, it was actually declared that the po'ouli bird was extinct.

It now seems that the birds had moved onto Moloka'i from Maui.

There have been no residents on Moloka'i ever since a volcano erupted in the year of 2027.

The team of entomologists had all agreed that the worm found in the fossils were exactly the same as the ones found to be killing the present-day birds and fish.

However, they have not found any worms in any of the fish fossils for some reason.

The worms must have died out millions of years ago, so how, and why, have they re-emerged after all this time?

"What we really need is a live *po'ouli* bird to examine, as they seem to be the only birds that are immune to the worms, probably due to their amazing resilience.

Their main food source is snails and spiders, which means that they must still have enough food, as the mosquitoes and flies leave the snails alone due to their shells, but I am not sure if it will be possible to catch a live bird.

That is down to Dr Williams and her team in Moloka'i."

By now, nearly all air travel around the world had been restricted to emergencies and for the world's air forces only, due to the situation with the insects clogging up the engines.

Over in Russia, one private oligarch had decided to ignore the restrictions. He and his family thought that it would be a good idea to take a trip to Niece, for a family holiday.

He had decided to travel at night-time, hoping that the authorities would not notice him.

The plane and his family of six took off from a small airport just outside St Petersburg, however, as he was flying towards the Pyrenees Mountains, the Russian air traffic controllers spotted an unauthorised plane taking off and alerted the Russian military.

Just as the private plane was over the Pyrenees Mountains, its engines developed problems. He radioed for help, but his radio was not working correctly.

By the time that two Russian military jets were about to make contact with him, his plane took a dive and it crashed into the mountains.

No one survived.

Dawn soon arrived on Moloka'i, the team had decided to take a look inside the nest before daylight would be in full swing.

They crept quietly, through the forest, and arrived at the base of the tree.

When they looked up, they could not see anything unusual.

Dr Williams gestured to the team that she was about to go up the ladder. Slowly and very carefully, the doctor climbed up the ladder with a butterfly net in hand, onto the platform in a tree that was opposite to where the nest was.

Somehow, one popular newspaper magazine had found out about the expedition to Moloka'i, and that they were going to attempt to capture one or two of the birds.

A very unpopular journalist from England, who worked for the newspaper magazine, but was working in Florida, had gathered about ten fellow journalists to join him on a large private jet that someone had offered him.

The private jet was in a hanger in Florida.

Without getting any clearance to fly, they all boarded the jet and set off towards Hawaii, so that they could then land and make their way to Moloka'i by boat to try to photograph the team of experts trying to collect the po'ouli bird.

The plane took off from Florida and headed towards Hawaii, it was quite a long flight, about nine hours, but as they were approaching Hawaii, the plane's engines were engulfed by a huge swarm of locusts, the pilot tried his best to control the plane, but he could not stop the engines from stalling.

The plane started to dive towards the sea.

There was nothing that the pilot could do, and sadly, the plane came crashing onto land and burst into flames. There were no survivors.

Just as Dr Williams was about to look inside the nest to make sure that the birds were still docile, there was an almighty bang, and the sky lit up.

Dr Williams shrieked, and she stumbled off the platform. She landed with quite a thud on the ground about fifteen feet below.

The rest of the team were also shocked and wondered what on earth was going on, they all thought that it was a thunderclap.

In the distance, they could see a huge fireball, and it looked like the forest was ablaze.

Dr Williams was helped up from the ground and although she was very shaken and a little dazed, she looked at her team and said,

"I am OK, but what on earth happened? The last thing that I remember was looking inside the nest, and here I am on the ground dazed and confused."

"We are not sure, but over there in the distance it looks like something had caused a huge fire, it could be a volcano erupting, as that is quite common in these islands," said a team member.

"No, that was definitely a plane crash. I have photographed them before," said the cameraman.

"A plane crash? That's impossible; all planes have been grounded," said Dr Williams.

"Whatever it was, I just hope that it did not frighten the birds. I must get back up there and check straight away, I am frightened that they may have flown away." she said.

After a short rest and a cup of coffee, Dr Williams carefully climbed back up the platform.

Slowly, she steadied herself and when she peered into the nest, amazingly, the birds seemed quite calm and unaffected by the commotion, then, just as Dr Williams was about to offer the net towards the nest, one of the birds suddenly appeared, and it flew straight into the net.

It was not angry to be inside the net, and it was not harmed at all, it seemed to be very calm.

As Dr Williams then looked inside the nest, she saw that there was one more bird, and to her amazement, there were also two birds' eggs.

She could not believe her eyes.

Dr Williams immediately called me to tell me about the explosion and fire, then she explained about the birds and the eggs, she then asked me if she should abort the mission.

I told her that it was imperative that they return with the birds and also the nest, and hopefully the eggs too, as they had not got the time to let the birds hatch and fledge.

As long as the two birds survive, it would be all right, as they were most important, but hopefully, the eggs would also be ok.

"These are the most precious birds and eggs in the world. I cannot emphasise just how careful we must be," said Dr Williams to her team.

Everything went to plan, the team managed to collect the birds, the eggs and also the nest.

The birds did not seem alarmed or frightened in any way, they were very docile, probably due to their amazing resilience.

They were then packed safely away inside a specially prepared container that had been brought with the team.

The team could feed the birds through special holes in the side of the container. It was a perfect mission.

Now the precious cargo had to be brought to me and my team in London, as soon as possible.

Then afterwards to Cape Town.

Dr Williams sent me a holographic video of the birds, the eggs and the nest inside the special containers.

I was extremely pleased, to say the least, as they looked very calm they could also monitor the birds 24 hours a day.

They found out later that it was a plane crash that they heard and saw.

It could have been a lot worse if the plane had crashed a mile further on.

Back in London, my team and I were getting closer to possibly solving the worm problem and the fact that the po'ouli birds found in Moloka'i seemed to be immune to the worms.

But how can we capitalise on this new information?

On hearing about the developments with the birds, President Hopwood arranged for her solar jet helicopter to take Dr Williams and her team safely back to London.

When Dr Williams and her team arrived, they were brought straight to my laboratory, along with the precious cargo.

I explained to Dr Williams that I wanted to take some DNA samples from the birds to try to reproduce it in the laboratory, as they were the only living birds that seem to be immune to the worms.

Before this happened, the professor and his assistant x-rayed the birds and also the eggs.

They could see no worms or anything unusual.

But they did see that the eggs were nearly ready to hatch.

I realised that I would soon have to do the very delicate procedure to extract the DNA samples from the birds, as I obviously did not want to harm or upset the birds in any way.

Meanwhile, all of the eggs that the team had collected so far were now vacuum packed and stored safely away in the special cool room.

They would all be soon heading for Antarctica, after the rest of the team could join them.

Back in London, a specially prepared British Naval jet hover boat was ready and waiting to take Professor Denton and his team, and also the po'ouli birds and the eggs, down to Cape Town.

However, after a lengthy discussion with Professor Denton, Dr Williams had decided to stay in London with the two birds and their eggs, as she wanted to make absolutely sure that they came to no harm.

She said that she felt obliged to nurture them until she was satisfied that they had come to no harm.

Professor Denton agreed that it was a sensible idea.

The Arctic explorer would be leaving Cape Town in about three days' time. Once all of the equipment and supplies were safely on board, the security surrounding was immense.

Meanwhile,

Supun and Hiruni had decided that their birds were healthy enough, they were still feeding and drinking normally.

However, strangely, they had still not started to sing again. They had noticed that there were hundreds of dead birds and fish, occasionally floating by them on their island, and they could not understand just what was going on.

They were very confused and extremely concerned about what was happening. They also realised that over the past few years, the climate around them had changed dramatically.

At one point, they had even considered travelling to one of the other islands in their group of islands just to see if they were having these same strange happenings.

After much discussion with each other, they decided to stay put and to see it out.

By now, the world leaders had declared a state of emergency throughout the entire world. Each country would have to look out for themselves.

Human deaths were still rising daily, with humans, as well as animals' bodies lying everywhere.

As soon as someone fell, the flies swarmed in from everywhere, and they laid their eggs.

It was a horrible sight, but there was nothing that anyone could do about it.

They tried to burn the bodies, but this proved to be difficult.

Farm animals were also affected by the flies and the mosquitoes. Cattle, horses, sheep, pigs and even snakes and other insects were affected.

In fact, nearly all wild and domesticated animals and insects were now dying off.

Soon it seemed that there would be nothing left on Earth, except the flies, locusts, mosquitoes, ants and rats.

At my laboratory in London, it was now time for the DNA to be extracted from the po'ouli birds.

Fortunately, they seemed to be thriving, amazing really when you consider what they have endured with their capture and very long journey of over 7,000 miles from Moloka'i to London.

Once I knew that the conditions were exactly right, I sedated one of the birds and then I very carefully managed to extract the samples that we needed. However, I was in a bit of a dilemma because I had told my team that what I really wanted to do was to sacrifice one of the birds to dissect it, although this was totally against my ethics as an ornithologist. I thought I would gain more information about how and why these remarkable birds had survived time after time.

Unsurprisingly, I was met with very strong opposition, especially from Dr Williams.

I tried to explain that if we knew how, or why, these birds could be immune to the worms, then we could possibly re-create their genes and inject them into the other birds' eggs.

Dr Williams argued strongly that they only had one male and one female bird, and if anything went wrong, then that would be the end of the species entirely.

A vote of whether to sacrifice one of the birds was taken by my team of scientists in a secret ballot, and the outcome was 5 votes for and 15 votes against.

I had lost my wish.

Chapter Seven
Only Time Will Tell

My examination of one of the po'ouli birds was a great success.

I had managed to extract all the DNA fluids and enzymes that I needed to find out how to replicate them, without harming the bird in any way.

Once the anaesthetic had worn off the bird, it calmly sat in its nest, along with his companion as if nothing had happened at all. Quite amazing.

Everybody in my team was waiting with bated breath for the results.

This could be the last chance to save the world.

I had my top team working on the DNA and I was confident that they could reproduce it soon.

Just as I was clearing away my laboratory equipment, I had the video call that I had been waiting for, for what seemed like an eternity.

"Hello, Professor Denton, I have some great news for you.

Look, here are the red worms, and the strange fish. Amazingly, they have survived the trip from over 7,000 feet down on the seabed; what amazing, yet deadly creatures they really are," said Professor Wilmot.

Professor Denton studied the video of the worms and the fish that were now in special tanks.

"Absolutely fantastic, well done.

I will pack a bag tonight, as I have now finished my DNA extraction. The British government has a special hover boat on standby waiting for us;

we will see you as soon as possible."

"That's wonderful. I cannot wait to show you how amazing these, until now, unknown fish and worms are.

The very next day, Professor Denton and a few of his team boarded the specially designed hover boat, along with the results of the DNA tests, and headed for Antarctica.

They arrived safe and sound seven days later, as they had to refuel along the way at the South Shetland Islands.

After unloading everything, they were taken to Professor Wilmot's laboratory.

The 'Sir David Matherson' Arctic explorer set sail for Cape Town soon after Professor Denton had left.

It took over three weeks before it arrived in Antarctica. However, it should have made that journey in less than two weeks.

En-route, the crew had to avoid thousands of dead birds that were floating in the ocean.

The captain reported it as follows:

"During the voyage down to Antarctica, it was at many times a very slow and hazardous journey.

You see, every now and then, we came across masses of dead birds. The numbers were astonishing.

What we saw initially looked like almighty huge black rafts, floating in the ocean; however, the black rafts occasionally took flight, as they were actually millions and millions of black flies that were feeding on the thousands of dead birds and fish.

"It was like something from a horror film. If we were not very careful, the birds and fish could have gotten tangled up in the propellers and that would have been disastrous for this very important voyage.

On the eighth night of our voyage, disaster struck.

"During the night, we encountered a severe storm, which came suddenly and without any warning.

"It was registered as a force 11 on the Beaufort scale, which is classed as 'A violent storm'. Our main concern was for the precious bird's eggs.

We were not concerned for the ship, as it has sailed in many storms like this before, some even worse.

"Although the eggs were extremely well packaged inside the special packaging, produced by Professor Hogan, some of my crew were babysitting them, day and night.

"The storm eventually passed us after an eight hour, nail-biting time. However, the very next morning, we encountered an even more potentially serious problem. It was at about 02.30 hours when suddenly the ship's engines stopped.

"My second in command called me in my cabin, to inform me that the engines had stopped and that he was not sure exactly what had caused it. I ordered him to gather a team of our best divers, and to have them suited up and await my arrival on the bridge. When I arrived, the team was ready for my orders.

"'Thank you for being so prompt; unfortunately, what I am going to ask you to do is not a very nice job. However, it is crucial that we get this ship back to doing the job that it has done so effectively for the past thirty-odd years.

"'After looking at the underwater cameras, it seems that the propellers are completely jammed up with what looks like some old fishing nets, and other objects that are tangled up within the nets.

"'Therefore, you must go below the ship to see just what has stopped the propellers and report back to me ASAP.'

"'Aye, aye, sir,' came the response.

"The men had special cutting equipment and also very powerful lights. It was now a very tense waiting game.

"After about ten minutes, over the radio, the men told me that there was indeed a massive fishing net that was tangled around all three propellers, and also, many dead fish, and even a couple of dead dolphins were stuck inside the nets.

"'It will take us quite a long time to clear the propellers,' they said.

"'Carry on as you see fit,' I told my men.

"It took my men over nine hours to remove the nets, and the fish, then we had to run tests on the engines to make sure that the propellers were not damaged. Amazingly, they were as good as new, so we set sail again, much to the relief of Professor Johnson and his team, who we had been in contact with the whole time in Antarctica. They were understandably extremely nervous about the very precious cargo.

"Once we had set sail again, this time I had put more officers on watch, and also I had deployed sonar scanning into the water."

In Antarctica, Professor Wilmot and Professor Johnson were at their wit's end, waiting for the birds to arrive.

However, it gave them both time to extract the DNA and other enzymes from the worms and the fish, which hopefully will help them to solve the problem.

When the ship finally arrived in Antarctica, a week late, time was now of the essence, it was all hands on deck to unload all the special equipment along with the birds and the eggs, and very carefully transport everything to a top-secret laboratory.

Professor Hogan was absolutely over the moon about how well the eggs were kept, considering what and where they have travelled from.

Meanwhile, Professor Denton and a couple of his team had gone on a trip to an island that was close to Antarctica, to see if it would be a suitable place to leave the birds if they are successful in incubating them.

Antarctica was now officially classed as a 'very safe zone', as no flies or mosquitoes could survive in its climate.

There is only one native insect that survives on Antarctica, that is an Antarctic midge, which actually spends half of its life in a frozen state.

They are quite remarkable insects, as they can survive for up to six months without oxygen.

Professor Hogan and his team had everything ready to go, as he and his team had practised the procedure multiple times for the past three months.

They had all previously worked day and night to make sure that there would be no mistakes or unforeseen problems.

He had previously stated that he did not wish to freeze the birds' eggs in liquid nitrogen, as he usually did, rather, he wanted to keep them at just above freezing point, and then he would monitor them hourly.

They had tested this procedure on a couple of chicken eggs, and he was very pleased with the results.

After a few days of tying up all the loose ends, I held a meeting for all the people in Antarctica. We are also going to broadcast a live special holographic link to President Hopwood, King William and the rest of the world leaders, to tell them about my results and most importantly, Professor Wilmot's results from our painstaking experiments.

I opened up the proceedings:

"Your Royal Highness, President Hopwood, distinguished ladies, gentlemen and fellow scientists.

As we are broadcasting here live from our secret laboratory in Antarctica, it gives me great pleasure to inform you all that the vital experiments that we have made from the living po'ouli birds have been very successful.

We have managed to replicate the DNA from the po'ouli birds, and we have also found the enzyme that I am sure makes the birds immune to the worms.

Now, comes the most important test that mankind has ever witnessed, to see if we can transfer the enzyme into a bird's egg and successfully incubate them.

Only time will tell.

However, my friend and colleague, Professor James Wilmot, has some very exciting news for you all.

I will now hand you over to Professor Wilmot who will explain his news."

"Thank you very much, Professor Denton, for that introduction, and many congratulations to you and your fantastic team, for your amazing work on the extremely important time for the future of the planet, and also for the rest of mankind.

What Professor Denton has failed to tell you all, is that about a week ago, my team and I sent a submersible down into the Arctic ocean, deeper than we have ever gone before, and amazingly, we found, and have also managed to capture, some of the living red worms that are the cause of the terrible devastation around the world.

Also, we discovered some, up until now, unknown species of fish that are, it seems, also immune to the red worms.

Now, hopefully, we can have our birds and fish back to where they belong. Only time will tell."

At this, there was an audible gasp from the eminent guests watching the video conference.

"Yes, you heard me correctly, it sounds impossible; we had no idea that these live worms existed, and that they were thriving under the ice-shelf.

When we found them, it was just pure luck, you see, we were only looking for the signs of those terrible earthquakes that happened here a few years ago.

That was when we came across the worms and some previously unknown fish purely by chance.

Amazingly, after some very delicate remote-controlled robot work by my amazing assistant, we managed to capture a few of the unknown species of fish that actually eat the red worms and apparently, they have no side effects at all.

My team and I have been working hard extracting the DNA from both the worms and the fish, with amazing results.

Dr Denton and I are now working away on experimenting on some of the live fish.

We hope to have the results within two weeks.

We will keep you informed of our progress.

Thank you all for listening."

All of the people spontaneously cheered and applauded Dr Wilmot and me, and my team, for our amazing work.

I later met up with Dr Khan, Professor Zack Hogan and Professor Wilmot privately in Professor Hogan's office, to discuss the next very important step for the birds' eggs.

After much discussion, we all agreed that they should first test the DNA on sparrows.

They would inject two sparrow eggs, then they will incubate them if they hatch, then they will feed them and allow the fledglings to grow into young adults under secure supervision.

If that is successful, afterwards, we had decided to take the birds to; 'Adams Island, which is a small island just to the south of New Zealand, as the climate there should be just about right in January/February.

This is the island that Professor Denton had previously visited earlier.

Adams Island is one of the nearest islands to Antarctica and the climate and conditions were deemed to be just right for the birds at that time of year, as due to the climate change, this island is now about seven degrees warmer than it was in the early 2000s.

My team and I had now started the delicate process of implanting the eggs.

First of all, I took two sparrow eggs, and I gently warmed them to the correct temperature.

Once that was done, I very carefully injected the eggs with the DNA sample and antibodies under a special x-ray microscope.

Although I had performed this sort of operation hundreds of times before, my hands were shaking, as I realized just how important this operation would be for the future of mankind.

The eggs were then put into an incubator, which was set at a precise temperature by Professor Hogan, after which it was a very tense waiting game.

Twelve days had passed when there was some movement inside the shells.

We all breathed a huge sigh of relief.

Two days later, the two young sparrows started to emerge from their shells, and they looked completely normal and healthy. Phew! So far, so good.

Dr Williams reported from London that the po'ouli chicks had hatched, and that they are also in perfect condition, also, she would be on her way to join us very soon in Antarctica.

Back in Antarctica, the sparrow chicks were now being drip-fed with a fine pipette.

The young chicks seemed to be growing at a normal rate and they looked very healthy.

Each day that passed, the birds grew a little more, and after a few days, they started to grow feathers.

When Dr Williams arrived, about two weeks later, we immediately held a meeting to discuss how we were going to release the fully grown sparrows into the wild, as we were concerned about the flies and mosquitoes. Although there were not many on Adams Island, there were some.

Dr Williams pointed out that the po'ouli birds on Moloka'i had survived, even though the island was infested with the insects. So, hopefully, the sparrows would survive there too.

It would be very risky even though no huge swarm of insects were reported on Adams Island.

The team then carefully packed the sparrows into a nesting box, as they were fully grown now, and then they set off to Adams Island.

They had all previously agreed that this would be a good place to leave the sparrows as it was once renowned for its birdlife.

Ironically, the bay that they had decided to land on was actually called 'Fly Harbour'.

The birds were both tagged, also, remote-controlled video cameras were set up all around the site.

Extremely fine netting was placed all around the nesting site to prevent any flies or mosquitoes invading the nest.

Strict security was put into place all around Adams Island to protect the birds.

"It is up to nature and science now, there was nothing else that we could do. We just hope that nature will take its course and there will be enough food for the sparrows to survive," said Dr Williams.

On Adams Island, there are a few native species of insects however, my team had set up a special feeding station above the nest to ensure that they had plenty to eat and drink.

We had even placed some temperature controls to ensure that if the weather did turn very cold, we could introduce some warm air.

Everyone was very concerned about leaving the sparrows alone on the island, but after much discussion, it was decided that it was the best thing to do.

If they had just looked after them in laboratory conditions, then it would not be a true test and results wouldn't be as effective.

"How long shall we leave them on the island?" asked Professor Hogan.

"That is a good question.

I believe that three months should suffice, but who knows? We have monitors and cameras all around them, and we will not interfere with the birds in any way, unless there are some unforeseen circumstances," said Dr Williams.

Meanwhile, Professor Wilmot and his team had managed to extract DNA from the strange fish, and they had delicately injected it into a variety of fish eggs, which were then fertilised by the male fish in the normal way. Everything was done under the strictest of conditions.

So far, things were looking good. The eggs were surviving at their normal growth rate, and in a few weeks' time, we will introduce them to the red worms.

Then it's a waiting game to see if they can survive.

Back in London, King William and the royal family had now been moved into a specially built underground bunker, along with some of their staff and advisors for protection. They had enough provisions to last up to one year.

Also, in New York, President Sandra Hopwood had moved from the White House Tower, together with her wife Hellen and her security team, to a top-secret location somewhere underground.

However, their children, Grace and Danny, were sent away to another secret site just in case one of the sites did not survive.

People all over the world were now desperate for some sort of normality to return to their lives.

Diseases and infections were now everywhere, and there was not enough medication available for everyone; it was a nightmare for most people.

Sadly, many older men and women were amongst the first people to perish along with many people that were on life-saving medication, due to a severe shortage in the production and distribution of the medicines and pills.

There were also huge food shortages all around the world, and many people were dying of starvation daily.

The chemically produced food was deemed to be a great success, however, sadly, they could not produce enough to distribute it to everyone in need.

Who would have known that if all the birds and fish disappeared, just how much devastation would be caused around the world?

The British Navy and the American Marines had now joined forces to build huge 'bubbles', as big as football stadiums; they were fitted with self-efficient solar-powered oxygen tanks and lighting. They held enough food and they had enough room for about 100 people in each one to last up to twelve months at a time.

In London, Russia and other large countries, thousands of old underground railway stations had been cleared out and fitted with survival equipment and enough oxygen and food was put in each station to last thousands of people for at least two years.

Similar work was done all over the world with the help of thousands of volunteers.

Everyone was now convinced that the end of the world was upon them.

But at last, the world was working together to help each other to survive.

The 'Mars Project', which was working to build huge liveable buildings on Mars, was stepped up, as the first trials were very successful.

It was now looking like a real possibility that Mars was the best option as a new home.

Also, huge energy-efficient rockets were nearly ready for the first groups of humans to be the first settlers on Mars.

Everyone was convinced that Mars was going to be the next planet to have humans as their inhabitants and within a few years, they would be able to grow crops and manufacture whatever they wanted with the new generation of 'Five-D printers'.

Thousands of young astronauts were now being trained at the 'Elon Musk' space centre, for lifetime missions to settle on Mars. It was definitely like something from the old sci-fi films, except this time, it was for real.

People from all around the world were also volunteering to be translators, as there would be many different nationalities that would be settling down on Mars.

Although most people worldwide now spoke a universal language based on English.

Chapter Eight
The Outcome

It has now been over three months, and the time had come to return to Adams Island to collect the sparrows and also to take them back to the laboratory for tests.

The surveillance of the sparrows was incredible.

They were acting just like normal birds, there was plenty of food and freshwater available for them.

The climate had been perfect, and there was no need to operate the climate control system.

Dr Williams asked Professor Denton if she could be the one to lead the team out to Adams Island to collect the birds from their nest, as she felt that it was mainly down to her from the start.

Everyone agreed. "If it wasn't for Dr Williams insisting on returning to Moloka'i when she did, then they would not be in this amazing position." I said

A few days later,Dr Willams and her team set off for Adams Island.

Meanwhile,

On 'Rumah' in the Cocos Keeling Islands, Supun and Hiruni had noticed that a few of their birds had started to sing a little again, but not all of them.

This was very encouraging to them both; they were hoping that eventually, all the birds would start to sing again as they had missed the bird song so much.

When Dr Williams and her team landed back onto Adams Island, they very carefully approached the nesting site.

Dr Williams started, very cautiously, to climb up onto the platform. She had with her a very fine butterfly net.

However, just as before, as she approached the nest, with her net, one of the sparrows suddenly flew out in front of her.

It made Dr Williams jump back a little, but luckily, she managed to catch the sparrow in her net, she then passed it down to her assistant.

She thought to herself that it was unusual behaviour as they had been so docile all along.

She then steadied herself to approach the nest for a second time, as she had noticed that the other sparrow was sitting quietly in the nest.

Carefully, she gently picked up the other sparrow, it was not happy to be picked up.

However, as she did so, she was in for the biggest shock yet, because as she gently picked up the sparrow, she saw that there were three birds' eggs in the bottom of the nest.

Dr Williams was so absolutely overjoyed, so much so, that she very nearly fell off her platform again.

The eggs had been hidden from the cameras all along by the sparrows sitting on them.

She quickly returned the sparrows back into the nest, then she climbed back down to the ground and straight away, she video called me to ask me for my advice.

I had actually been watching the whole event live, and I had seen what had happened on a monitor.

I, too, was elated. I then advised Dr Williams to come straight back to Antarctica, as I did not want to jeopardise the experiment, which had gone amazingly well so far.

Professor Wilmot called Professor Denton to bring him up to speed regarding the injected fish.

He was pleased to report that up to now, the fish were behaving as normal fish.

So far, the red worms have had no effect on them at all.

Back at the Natural History Museum in London, the leading archaeologist had his report ready regarding the worms.

He sent his report via hologram to the team in Antarctica and also to the world leaders.

It read as follows:

This is the report of Professor Donald G. Peterson, BSc, BA, MA, MSc, PhD.

After extensive investigations regarding the deadly worms, it is my conclusion that the very same worms were eradicated during the Jurassic period; however, this event may have also happened in the Cretaceous period also, and possibly during more recent times, for example about two thousand years BCE as the reports from the Egyptians had stated.

The reasons why it happened? We don't fully understand; however, due to the climate changes and the severe weather conditions, i.e., terrible droughts and flooding all over the world, followed by devastating earthquakes and tsunamis, I am convinced that it was due to when Antarctica suffered that terrible earthquake, back in 2029.

Amazingly, due to the recent amazing discovery in Antarctica by Professor Wilmot and his team, it is my belief that deep inside the Earth's crust, under the Arctic ice shelf, and possibly in other places in the deep oceans, there are pockets of millions, possibly billions, of the tiny red worm eggs that must have been lying dormant in the frozen temperatures.

Possibly, due to the severe earthquakes etc., they have somehow managed to surface from deep within the Earth's crust and incubated, and re-surfaced again after hundreds of thousands of years.

This must have also happened at least twice before many, many years ago.

It also seems that there appears to be something in a bird's and some fish anatomy, that when the birds and the fish eat the worms, they somehow latch onto their intestines, and sadly, the birds and fish are then doomed. Why, and how? I do not understand.

Therefore, I conclude that 'this world disaster' actually started over two hundred million years ago, during the Jurassic period and has occurred at least twice since then.

It is amazing that Dr Williams and her team managed to find possibly the only bird in the world, which remarkably, in fact, was thought to be extinct, that it is resilient to the worms.

The good news is that the birds must have eventually replenished somehow, so now we just need to discover how.

The same goes to Professor Wilmot and his team for that amazing discovery of the strange fish and the red worms.

Without those two discoveries, the world would have been doomed.

After we had all watched the report, there was complete stunned silence. Then, quite spontaneously, everyone broke out in a round of applause.

Dr Williams then said.

"What an amazing report, it makes complete sense, that is exactly as Professor Denton had thought, but we would have never known about the worms before as they are so tiny.

The worms could have also had something to do with the disappearance of some species of dinosaur, something so small, yet it has caused such devastation, so who knows?"

Two months had now passed when Dr Williams and her team returned to Adams Island, as they had seen on the remote-controlled cameras the young sparrows hatch, and grow just like normal birds they were now ready to fledge.

Dr Williams then carefully captured all of the sparrows, so that she could test them for the worms.

My team managed to scan and x-ray the birds.

After a very tense few hours in the laboratory, I announced that all the sparrows were complete, worm free!

I knew that it is still early days, and we must not get too excited about the findings, as we know that unforeseen complications can arise if you get too complacent.

I then reported our findings to the world leaders, and they all agreed that we should do further experiments with other species of birds and take them to various parts of the world to see if the results were the same, just to make sure that it was not just a one-off.

Back in Antarctica, Professor Wilmot had some bad news.

He explained;

"When we tested the fish, at first, there were no signs of the red worms, however, now, three months later, sadly most of the fish have got the red worms in their guts and they are dying.

"But it appears that not all the varieties of fish that we were testing have. We are going to do further testing."

Professor Wilmot, along with Professor Zack Hogan, held a meeting to discuss what to do next with the fish.

After further extensive tests on various fish, they found out that when they gave the oily fish (pelagic fish) the DNA, the worms died inside the fish, and the fish seemed to be acting like normal fish.

However, when the non-oily fish were given the DNA, they were still dying off because of the worms.

(Non-oily fish only have oil in their livers, and they also have various toxic substances throughout their bodies.

The pelagic fish have oil inside their belly cavity and around their guts.)

Professor Wilmot's team of scientists worked day and night, testing various enzymes and non-toxic chemicals.

Two months had passed when they had a 'eureka' moment.

As one of the team was testing various enzymes, she noticed that one of the worms dissolved completely however, the fish itself was not affected at all.

Professor Wilmot immediately ordered further tests on other species of fish with the enzyme, and the results were the same.

Many, many, more tests were extensively done and it was declared a great success.

The world health organization gave the green light on a new enzyme, as all of their tests were positive.

The British government immediately ordered the production of the new enzyme in huge numbers, to be distributed worldwide.

After further tests on the enzyme, they found out that just adding the enzyme to water in the tanks of fish worked, without actually injecting it into the fish.

Under normal conditions, it would take many years of testing to allow any non-natural chemicals to be introduced into the world oceans and rivers however, all of the top scientists and world leaders gave us the go-ahead to continue.

This was going to be absolutely amazing to distribute the enzyme into the rivers, lakes and even the seas. It is going to take many years to get the fish and the birds back to what they used to be, but at least we seemed to have a solution.

Eventually, the new enzyme was taken way down into the area on the very bottom of the Arctic Ocean, where the worms were coming out, and within six months, they had all disappeared.

Once we had made the discovery about the red worms at the bottom of the ocean, divers looked at many more underwater sites that had suffered earthquakes and they found that under the ocean surrounding the Galapagos Islands, there were the red worms, just as in Antarctica.

The enzyme was distributed around the crack in the seabed and it was monitored daily.

After about six months, the red worms had completely disappeared.

Twelve months have now passed since our last bird and fish trials, and each trial since has been very successful.

No worms have been found in any of the birds or fish.

The bird and fish populations now seem to be flourishing again.

However, it seems that some species of fish and birds sadly did not survive. The tests had been deemed a great success.

Back in India, the group of beekeepers that had covered a twenty-five-mile area with netting and also planted thousands of flowers and various plants, to help save the bees, had also had great success keeping thousands and thousands of bees alive.

This would prove to be essential for the whole world once everything was back to normal.

Once we were absolutely certain that the bees were not in any danger, they were gradually introduced back into the wild. Gradually, the bee population continued to grow and to flourish again.

Myself, Dr Williams, Professor Wilmot and Professor Hogan, along with the apiarists in India, were all celebrated as heroes worldwide.

Although we all dismissed the accolades, as we all said that we were just doing the jobs we had trained for.

Plans were made to slowly reinstate as many birds to each country as soon as possible.

Also, new chemical-free insecticides that were tested were used and they were also a great success with absolutely no effect on humans or animals.

The terrible plagues of flies, mosquitoes and locusts were now under control. Mars astronauts were taking birds, bees and even fish to Mars, hoping that they would survive, so far, they were doing great.

New buildings were built and it was looking like it would be a great success.

Eventually, they wanted to build a whole new ecosystem on Mars, and hopefully, man would look after it much better than they have done back on Earth.

It will take about twenty years or so for things to 'normalise'. However, one of the best things that came out of this terrible disaster was that it brought the people of the world together as one, especially the world religions, and everyone from then on was committed to really caring for our wonderful planet.

Professor Zac Hogan was allowed to keep the secret laboratory in Antarctica along with Professor Wilcox just in case.

Eventually, they would restock it with birds' eggs from all the birds of the world, just in case there was ever another disaster.

Ants too had played their part in the eradication of the worms, as due to excessive colonies of ants worldwide multiplying in huge numbers, they were eventually able to feast on the rest of worms that were still around.

A safe insecticide that was developed was able to eradicate most of the locust swarms and to keep them under control. The flies, due to not being able to feed on all those corpses around, eventually reduced to their normal state.

The rat problem too was now under control, and a completely new sterilising system had been discovered, which was proving to be very successful.

Although there were many more climatic disasters worldwide, people were much more prepared for any event.

Meanwhile,

As for Supun and Hiruni, well, their birds all ended up singing again, this time, even louder than before.

Their birds had never actually been infected by the worms at all, possibly due to them being on the floating platforms.

However, they must have had some inner sense of a problem with the birds elsewhere, as that would account for their strange behaviour.

The rest of the world was oblivious to 'Rumah' Island, and Supun and Hiruni were completely oblivious to the devastating disaster that nearly wiped out all the rest of the birds and fish.

In Antarctica, Professor Wilmot and his team have set up many seismic detectors, so that even the slightest earthquake will be thoroughly examined and monitored.

To date, the worms have not returned since, but if they do, there is a confidence that the birds and fish will be safe.

Professor Zack Hogan was also instrumental in helping to solve the problem of the melting icebergs with amazing success.

Dr Williams and Dr Khan agreed to work together to help with various diseases and infections of people and animals worldwide.

Professor Denton sadly passed away just a few years after his great achievement.

A new university was built in his and his late wife, Diane's, honour for their great work.

At last, the birds were singing again, and it was all thanks to the wonderful *po'ouli* bird.

The End